# The Origin

## Elle Klass

# The Origin



**Author's Disclaimer**

# REALM WALKER

**Books in the Realm Walker Series**
In the Shadows
The Land of Lost Souls
Hidden Passages
The Ring of Betrayal

**Other Realm Walker Companion Books**
The Origin: Marya's Journal

**Realm Walker World Books – coming soon!**
Love at Frost Bite
Accidental Ghost: Soul Catcher Vol.1

**Other Young Adults Series**
The Bloodseeker
Zombie Girl
Hidden Journals
Baby Girl

# 1

## In and around the 13th century

I glanced at my parents sleeping soundly. My father's arm draped over my mother's middle. "I love you," I whispered, then tossed the satchel over my shoulders and escaped into the night. Everything I needed was tucked into the lining so as not to be found.

A small tree emerged from the ground. I pressed my hand gently over the top. "This is for you." Whispers carried through the treetops as I stole away from my home. The distant squawking of dragons pulsated in my head, and I wasn't sure if they were really out, flying over Canida, or if they were phantom sounds.

"Davi," I whispered, nearing his family's trella or home. Not seeing him, I pressed my back against a tree and waited. Twisting my long, dark, twin braids together nervously, I tied them in a knot. *Make haste,* murmured through the chilly air, reminding me I needed to move. There was no time for Davi.

I glanced one last time at his family's trella then pushed off the tree. It was my mission more than his. He was going for adventure and support. I'd continue the mission alone and let him sleep. Within a few minutes, footfalls crunched the leaves and grass. I spun around, my hand on a small knife hanging from my belt. Davi. Letting out a sigh, I waited as his long, dark braid bounced against his chest with each footfall.

He'd been my best friend since we were kids and times were peaceful. It was almost impossible to remember what peace felt like. Each day blasted with the sounds of war, smell of flames, and the sight of winged creatures as they circled the border of Canida. All the death and destruction seemed a waste over something I barely understood. 'One day, when you're grown, everything will make sense' my parents parroted, but I didn't think any of it ever would. It was time for someone to end it all.

Davi was always late, no matter what time he needed to be somewhere. "Today wasn't the time to be late. We have to move,"

I chided him. Spinning on my heel, I marched forward.

He caught up. "My father stirred. I stole out the window, nearly fracturing a bone." The words rolled off his tongue with ease.

I paused, studying his features; straight serious mouth, never-ending blue in his eyes, and wrinkles pressed into his forehead. He meant his words, but to me they were an excuse for his tardiness. In my life, I'd heard many excuses from him. His window was all of a meter off the ground. I gave him the 'I-don't-believe-you' look and started walking again.

"Really." He stumbled ahead, catching up. "I tossed my bag out first then stumbled over it. I'm OK."

Ignoring his plea for empathy, I stressed, "We need to be hidden by daybreak."

The iridescent blue sarcantha flowers illuminated our path and the solaflies buzzed around us, shining in an array of colors. It reminded me we were never alone. All life in Aradia was one with the elf population. That was how I extracted fruit from the Serenity Tree – the lifeblood of Aradia.

Its trunk surrounded by water as its thick roots tangled, sinking below the surface. Its branches dropped, filled with bundles of silver leaves. Once a year, in the dead of the cold, it bloomed. Large, yellow, five petal blooms trimmed in gold made a brilliant display. Its fruit, painted gold, dropped into the waters below.

Legend had it the Serenity Tree signified all life. Its roots dug deep below the surface and spread through the dirt of each and every realm, supplying the nutrients all life needed for survival. It was the largest tree anywhere. Its thick trunk thicker than my families trella.

"Giseppa be with us," Davi said, referring to Queen Giseppa. Serenity Tree wasn't the only thing significant in elf history, and sometimes that history overlapped other realms and peoples such as Giseppa's story. According to fae/elf lore, Queen Giseppa grew tired of King Herard's harsh tactics on the fae people and, in protest, disappeared into the Aradian forest.

The forest was a place fae were sent for punishment and death. No one ever returned. King Herard mourned her the rest of his days. She hadn't died, nor had those who were banished. They lived amongst the trees and life, adapting, and created a new type of kingdom where everyone was equal. Queen Giseppa let her hair grow, never cutting it again, to honor the trees and their branches. The other fae followed her lead and, to this day, no elf cut their hair. Over generations, the banished fae became a new subspecies with their own distinct characteristics – elves. The elven and fae eventually made a truce and they existed in peace as neighboring realms until the great war…

# 2

Sier was a realm that spanned the highlands to the prairies. Ice dragons lived at the highest peaks, fire dragons below them, and lycans covered the prairies. When the Dragon King's son became deathly ill. A courier was dispatched immediately to Aradia. Elves were known for many skills, such as designing fabrics made from trees in Aradia, telepathy, and healing remedies. People from all realms came to Aradia when they, or someone they knew, suffered any type of illness.

When the dragon courier arrived, the elves dispatched their best elf healer and his apprentice, wasting not a moment. As elves, they took pride in their healing remedies and abilities. It wasn't elf-style to turn away when help was needed. Not that much reason existed at the time to turn away the dragons.

The fastest way to Sier is through the prairie lands and the lycans' territory. The team never made it, as the lycans shot down the dragon carrying the elves with an arrow laced in vampire blood; the one thing that will kill a dragon – an agonizing death. The lycan rebellion started the day the dragon, the elf, and his apprentice died by lycan teeth and claws; their bodies ripped apart.

I had trouble blaming the lycans even though every part of me wanted to. I knew the conditions they lived under. The Dragon King treated them as the lowest life form and the lycans became fed up to the point they did desperate things, such as kill two innocent elves.

They made a stand to no longer be second class citizens and took it upon themselves to divide the land. They call the prairies and low woods Canida. No longer do they serve the king. Of course, the king wasn't happy about their decision.

At first, I was furious with the lycans. The death was on their hands. but, knowing how they were treated, I couldn't justify hating them even though they were responsible for killing the elves. It was the Dragon King. If he'd treated them better, listened to their woes, made a truce with them, given them the lands they asked for, they wouldn't have needed to kill anyone.

Angered by the death of one of his dragons, and the elves carrying the remedy to cure his only son who will one day rule Sier, the king worked into a rage. He sent fire dragons over Canida, burning the tall grasses and wildflowers. The flames rose into the sky in a seemingly never-ending fire. Ash and soot rained down on Aradia, which borders Canida. The fires threatened to burn Aradia; a land thick with forests and flora. They grew closer each day.

It was never an elf fight but, losing our own, it became a war as elves fought back. Plants whipped and tangled around the lycans, squeezing the life from them. Their bodies tossed over the border by large branches, others pushed into the soil where new life would burst forth. It wasn't enough, nor did it make any elf feel better. Justice may have been served, but in a war there was no justice, only lives lost and others destroyed.

The elves, filled with disdain for lycans, made a pact with the vampires, whose hatred for the lycans was boundless. An army of them stealing through the night from Drakonia (their realm) through the area where all realms connected, a harsh land filled with treacherous terrain and pitfalls. Each loaded with weapons and swords coated in silver; the one thing that will kill a lycan.

The battle didn't stop, nor was anyone deterred. The lycans made a pact with the trolls in Verboten. As miners and crafters, the trolls worked closely with the lycans who build. They needed each other and the trolls stepped into the war. Crafting weapons laced in lycan blood and saliva which kills vampires, and arrows dipped in vampire blood, the one thing that will kill a dragon. Verboten and Drakonia border each other, and trolls would steal into the realm during the daylight hours on kamikaze missions to drain vampires of their blood.

Whispers passed through the trees and flora that division was sewing amongst the fae. Some sympathetic to the lycans, others sympathetic to the elves, yet most stayed neutral, complaining this wasn't their war. Rage boiled inside me, and decisive action needed to be taken. It was time for the war to end and, clearly, the Dragon King was at fault. He would pay the price to end the great war.

I'd plotted the path that I felt would be best, considering the options. Taking the route where all the realms met would be too treacherous, with hidden valleys, mountains covered in sharp rock, swamps with poisonous serpents, hideous dark nymphs with their razor sharp teeth and the possibility of vampires. That option off the table, I chose to go through each realm.

# The Origin

Another route to Navarin would take us through the Karanak woods and the capital of Aradia – Aradin. It would be populated, and we'd stand a good chance of being found out. All elves spoke with the plants telepathically and there was no way to control the plants' chatter. To avoid the plants and elves, we had one other route through the darklands. A densely wooded place surrounded by thorns and brambles.

No elf went into the darklands, but I didn't see another way. If the trees spoke, we'd surely be found. If we were seen, we'd be returned to our families. I didn't set out on this journey with any belief it would be easy, but I wasn't going home yet either.

When we came to a fork I stopped, and Davi continued to the right toward the Karanak woods. He turned and walked back, noting I wasn't beside him. Studying my face, he stopped and shook his head. "No. It's too dangerous. We can't."

There were stories how no one ever returned from the darklands, and babies were stolen from their homes by the hideous, vile creatures who inhabited them. Honestly, I didn't know anyone who'd actually dared go into the darklands. Most of what I heard, I didn't believe. They were part of Aradia and safer, despite the rumors of disappearances, large, venomous creatures with fangs, and poisonous plants. "Maybe for you. You can go on and get caught. I'll take my chances."

He twisted his face in frustration, understanding how stubborn I could be. "It's a wasteland covered in thorns. You won't survive. We can get through the Karanak woods without being spotted."

I ignored his pleading and stepped left at the fork towards the darklands. "They'll spot you," I called. If another elf didn't catch us, the plants would whisper their whereabouts, carrying the message: *They entered the darklands.* Not a single elf would follow, and the plants of the darklands didn't reveal their secrets.

Crunching leaves announced he was jogging to catch up to me. There was no talking me out of anything. Once my mind was made up, it was a done deal.

He kicked the fallen leaves and they spiraled into the air and fell around us. "We could get lost in there, wander for days and starve."

I snorted, radiating confidence on the outside, but inside a bundle of confusion and doubts. "Or we could march through and enter Navarin on the other side."

The iridescent, blue-glowing sarcantha plants ended a few meters from the treacherous trees and bushes surrounding the darklands. I plucked a bunch and stuffed them into my satchel. The sun climbed over the thorny mess. Planting myself on a log, I opened the satchel and grabbed a sweet, juicy pika. I had a plan, but it wasn't fully plotted. Large thorns like spikes climbed the tree trunks; small plants with sharp, pointed leaves and dull, gray blooms, and brambles weaved through leaves and trunks. *How would we get to the other side? Was the entire darklands like the gnarly trees protecting it?* If so, we wouldn't make it.

Davi collected a pika from the satchel and sank his teeth in for a bite as he studied the thorny, intimidating wall of plants. "I don't think we can get through."

Determination might as well have been my name. I'd find a way. Studying the plants, I didn't see an area we could sneak through without getting cut, but didn't give up the chance there was one. There had to be. I grabbed Davi's hand and squeezed for extra magic to communicate with the plants of the darklands. Regular Aradian plants weren't a challenge, but the ones of these mysterious and treacherous woods I knew nothing about. When I opened my eyes, nothing had changed.

"They aren't going to let us in." He stuffed the last bite of pika into his mouth. "We might as well turn back," he mumbled with a mouthful of fruit.

Sinking my teeth into the fruit, I stepped forward. Pika juice rolled down my throat and the sweet flesh of the fruit was soft on my tongue. "Nonsense. We're elves."

The brambles and dull, gray flowers unwound from the trees and bushes, twisting towards me as I moved forward. They wound around my feet loosely. I stepped over them and they moved again, running up my leg. At this point, most elves would leave, run scared, but not me. I was scared, but not about to run. The success of the mission depended on me being brave. I held to my belief this was the path we needed to take.

Davi rushed toward me, knife in hand, his face twisted in aggression.

Horrified he was about to cut the gnarly brambles and branches from my legs, I screamed. "No! Elves don't harm plants," I chided. "They're inspecting me, deciding if I can enter." I made that up, but it made sense. Plants were like that.

He stepped back as more brambles moved towards him. His pulse quickened as the brambles moved over his ankles and drifted up his leg. Careful not to move, he dropped the knife, showing he meant no harm. The brambles receded without drawing blood.

I couldn't help but roll my eyes at Davi. Reaching the barrier of treacherous plants, centimeters from a thorn large enough to go through my neck, vines unwound from the trees and wrapped around my body like rope. The trees parted as the vines pulled me in, managing to do it with such precision I slipped past the massive thorn without a scratch.

"Marya!" Davi screamed.

# 3

I stumbled forward as the vines unwrapped from around my middle, spiraling back to where they came. It happened so quickly there wasn't time to react or fight them off. I was determined that cutting through the darklands was the only route, even if I didn't make it out alive. At least I would have tried.

Blackness darker than a starless night surrounded me. I couldn't see a thing. It was as if someone stuffed me into a closet and locked the door. I groped the cool moist earth below my fingertips then pushed upwards, only to be knocked in the rear. Falling forward, I face planted from the weight of the body that slammed into me. Lifting my head upward, I smelled a familiar, earthy scent. "Davi."

"Marya. We're alive." His voice a stammer of fear.

I grabbed for his hand. Together we stood, fingers laced together for comfort. I glanced upward, searching for a break between the canopy of leaves, a small glimmer of light. It was daylight before the vines thrust us into the dark cave of trees. There wasn't a single sign of light from above.

"It's too late now… to go back. Take the route through the Karanak woods," Davi said, reminding me we were now stuck inside the darkness of the forest no elf dared to enter.

It was my choice. I'd make it work. Fear snaked up my legs and over my spine then I remembered the bunch of sarcantha I'd stuffed into my satchel. My fingers fumbled inside the satchel, finding the flowers on top where I left them. I held them out and swallowed hard. The rumors were true. An eight-eyed creature stared at us as if we were its dinner. "Davi," I whispered.

His back close to mine, he turned and let out a whimper.

"You see it too?" I couldn't hide the stammer of nerves in my voice.

He nodded, as if I could see him. If he wasn't so close, I wouldn't have known he'd nodded at all. "There's more," he said, finding his voice.

I tossed sarcantha petals to the right and left, illuminating a tall, humanoid creature with wings and another with feelers jetting from the top of its head.

The eight-eyed creature moved forward. Its several legs carrying an elongated abdomen. Six, I counted six legs. Two in front, two in the middle, and two in back. Its voice female and its words strung out and slow: "Why have you entered the darklands?" it said, without moving its mouth. Did it have a mouth? Light from the sarcantha glowed from the ground, the creature's face mostly shadowed.

This creature, whatever it was, displayed intelligence. I stumbled over my words: "I'm Marya and I… we…" Finding my confidence and gaining control of my tongue, I spat the words out: "We're on our way to Sier to stop the great war."

A chorus of chuckles enveloped us. There were more than three creatures. It sounded like several. "Two young elves going to stop the great war. Others before you have tried to save their own. You will die," the eight-eyed female creature said in slow but punctuated words.

Davi whispered, "I warned you. They're going to kill us."

I shoved my elbow in his side, warning him to close his mouth. The eight-eyed creature spoke again: "It's not us you need fear. We won't kill you. It is the others outside the darklands."

The words resonated in my head. Yes, there were some who would take pleasure in killing us, but surely not elves. Until the great war, Aradia was a beautiful place to live. It felt safe until my brother was killed; the elven apprentice sent to heal the Dragon King's son. Most of him was recovered and buried near our family's trella. A small tree sprouted from the soil, marking the spot of his grave. That is the elven way. When one dies, the energy creates new life.

"What do you mean?" I asked.

"You are young," the creature said in her punctuated words as she walked around us. Her eight-eyes inspecting us. "You traveled all night, and it is a long journey through the darklands. Come, we have food and a place you can rest."

The sarcantha started to lose its glow as we followed her. "Do you have light?" I asked, my voice sounding small and insignificant.

The creature didn't respond but, from behind, a bright light cast a glow on the path ahead. I peeked over my shoulder to see several insects following us, some more elf in appearance than others. The light glowed from the tall humanoid's wings, spread wide and shining like a star. "Thank you."

Various sizes and types of plants I didn't recognize clumped in bunches as we followed a well-worn path until we arrived at a large, wooden trella. It was round, vertical logs and vines held the sides together, and more vertical logs made the roof. It came together at a point. Light shone from between the logs.

Inside, wax lights glowed from tables. It looked like a cafeteria. Several creatures stopped what they were doing. Their conversations dropping into a void as we entered, as if we were the enemy, and they might give away battle secrets.

My breath caught as I studied each creature. Most were large insects with antenna, thorax, and exoskeletons; others four-legged animals with scaly skin, and one legless that slithered close to us. Its forked tongue shot from its mouth, nearly smacking Davi in the face. "Elvesss don't belong," it said, as it slithered away into a dark corner.

Davi squeezed my hand so hard I was sure he'd stopped the circulation in my arm. "If you show us back to Aradia, we will never come back."

"Shush!" said the eight-eyed creature. "Sit." It lifted a leg and pointed to a log bench and a table.

# The Origin

Obediently, we sat, both of us too scared to do anything different than what they asked. We'd never seen or heard of such creatures. A thick humanoid with antennae and a blue exoskeleton set two bowls of something steaming on the table in front of us.

"Eat," the eight-eyed creature said as she returned to us.

The steaming bowl had a thick, creamy, tan liquid with chunks in it. I dipped a wooden spoon into the bowl and sipped, surprised at how good it was.

The humanoid with bright wings dropped a blanket over the eight-eyed female's abdomen and, before our eyes, she changed. Her eight eyes became two. Her front legs became arms and back legs became regular legs with flesh. Her abdomen elongated. I blinked in disbelief. Long, dark, straight hair parted as pointed ears grew from the sides of her head.

"You're elf?" Davi said, not hiding that he was as stunned as me.

"No, We are elvarin. Our ancestors lived peacefully in the land of Aradia. When the first fae were banished here, they lived amongst us, bred with us, and gained the ability through blood to shift partially into insects, and even gained the ability to speak telepathically with plants, insects, and reptiles."

I glanced at the odd creatures. Shift partially – that explained why some were complete, large insects and others looked more elf. It also explained how elves had the ability to communicate with plants. "That's how we communicate with plants."

She nodded.

"Yesss. The fae bred with those here that didn't look like usss," the legless creature said from the dark corner, expressing his disgust of the fae.

"You mean those who shift?"

"No, those who shift into insectsss and reptilesss. They don't mind those who shift into a creature with fur, four legsss and a horn on the center of itsss head, or a brightly colored bird that spitsss water, or even a creature who livesss below the sssea adorned in toxic scalesss," the legless one criticized as he came out of the dark corner. His head thick and shaped like a sideways square.

"So you hide here?" Davi asked.

The former eight-eyed creature responded: "No. Giseppa and the fae who came with her drove the elvarin to the darklands, little by little. They didn't approve of our ancestors' appearance, feared their differences. Called them hideous monsters. They burned their trellas, villages, and gardens until there was nowhere else for them to go. Giseppa wouldn't dare enter the darklands."

# The Origin

I was mortified, but not shocked. The fae were well known for their uppity attitude, always putting themselves first. I was surprised that Giseppa was as bad as the rest. Elves are taught to admire and worship her like a god. She is the mother of elves and they aren't taught about these creatures whose home was stolen. We'd been lied to our entire lives. Not only had the fae stolen Aradia from the elvarin, they stole their name too, shortening it.

The humanoid with the feelers on his head spoke, his voice filled with sadness: "Elven children born with any of our traits were brought to the edge of the darklands and left to die or be rescued by our kind."

I couldn't hide the horror on my face. That explained the baby-napping tales. Disgust pushed up my throat, threatening to escape as vomit. "That's the most awful thing I've ever heard."

The former eight-eyed creature stood, her eyes shifting over Davi and me, studying us. "You two are different. The darklands trust you, therefore we trust you. I'm Chrishta. If you need anything, let me or Matthia know." She pointed to the humanoid with the luminescent wings.

My eyelids grew heavy and everything else after that blurred until a tapping woke me. I stirred in the darkness. A dim light shone from a table across the room, spreading over an exit. This wasn't the cafeteria, but another room. I wasn't even sure if it was in the same trella. Davi snored quietly beside me. To avoid waking him, I carefully sat up and crawled off the mat. Pushing onto my legs, I strolled to the exit.

The steady tapping continued in my ears. There were two burning waxes on the table. I assumed one for me and one for Davi. They were in wooden holders with a ring big enough for a finger. I looped my finger through the ring and exited into a hallway. It spilled into a larger room with a balcony.

Matthia rested against the wooden rails of the balcony, his wings flat on his back. He turned his head when he heard me. I joined him, leaning my arms against the railing.

"Did the rain wake you?" he asked, as if reading my mind.

I held out my hand but didn't feel any rain. The darklands were moist, but if the water didn't fall directly into the darklands and simply rolled off the thick canopy, where did it go?

"You won't feel the water," he said, eying my hands held over the rail as if to catch it.

"Where does it go?"

"It rolls off the waxy leaves and into trenches where it flows into the darklands as a stream. Some will soak into the ground."

Despite his insect wings, he was quite beautiful, with pointy elf ears, dark hair in many braids that rolled over the top of his head and hung over his back and wings. His profile displayed his chiseled features. "Are you all born here?"

He took his eyes off whatever he was watching and glanced my way. "No. My parents left me outside the darklands. The trees pulled me in and Chrishta found me. My wings gave away what I am from my birth."

My heart broke. How could parents leave their own child. Did they ever think about him, or was he dead to them? It was difficult to imagine an elf abandoning their child. "Do you remember them at all?"

"No. I was too young. They did manage to hide me for several months."

"I'm really sorry."

"I'm not. The elvarin are my family."

His words gave me little comfort to imagine how awful the fae were, and maybe some elves too. Matthia wasn't old enough to be a child of our ancestors, so the practice of leaving babies outside the darklands still existed. It was barbaric.

Chrishta made sure we ate again before leaving. She and Matthia escorted us to the path.

In her elfin form, she handed Davi a glowing bag that spread enough light we could see a few meters in front of us. "Use this for light. Follow the path straight. Don't look left or right, nor turn your head to see behind," she said, her words filled with warning.

"Why?" I asked.

Her elf eyes met mine. "You may see something that you won't be able to unsee," Chrishta responded in drawn-out, punctuated words.

"Take this," Matthia said, handing me a chunk of bark. "This is bark from the sacha tree. Suck on it, don't bite it, and certainly don't swallow it."

Davi got a beautiful glowing bag and I got bark. Plants had all types of purposes, but it wasn't pretty or sweet smelling. "What is it's use?" I asked.

"You will know when the time is right. Keep it close," Matthia warned, as if it was of great importance.

# 4

The patter of rain on the canopy of leaves dropped off, followed by a persistent quiet. So quiet, I heard my own thoughts.

"Do you believe all that stuff?" Davi asked, as if the silence was getting to him as well.

*Did I?* I wasn't sure. It was difficult to think of an elf leaving their own child outside a forest everyone feared. It was tough to swallow that creatures such as Matthia and Chrishta existed and, furthermore, asked to believe the great Giseppa wasn't the person elves thought. We were taught to worship her, yet how could I after what I'd heard? Their tales offered a speck of doubt and my gut had to at least believe in the possibility of their words. "Yeah. Have you ever seen anything like them?" The look on his face answered the question. "Neither have I. And why don't elves go into the darklands? All the scary stories, right. Stuff made up to keep us out."

"I guess," he said with hesitation.

I believed the elvarin. It wouldn't help them to make stuff up, and it answered the questions – even the ones about baby snatching. "We've been lied to our entire lives. What other things have they lied about?" Talking was keeping my mind off the temptation to look left, right, and behind me. It also filled the silence.

"Maybe trolls were fae too," Davi joked.

"That's a funny thought, but it would answer the question about why they have tails and plumage."

We laughed and, once our laughter died down, it was us and the eerie silence again. The light spread far enough we could see the path ahead and the shadows of trees, but we didn't dare move our eyes off the trail.

Davi leaned towards my ear and whispered, "I feel like we're being watched."

I shared that feeling. Even before the rain stopped, I hadn't felt we were alone. "Me too." I was dying to look, but I kept my eyes straight ahead. *Chrishta was nice, but what other things lived in the darklands?*

# The Origin

A slight rumble filled the dead space. I glanced at Davi, careful to keep my eyes focused on him. "Let's eat. It's been hours." I stopped directly on the path and dropped to my butt. Opening my satchel, I weeded around until I found another pika.

He dropped next to me on the dirt path and took the sweet fruit.

A branch cracking echoed in my ears. As a reaction, I nearly looked to my right then consciously reminded myself: *Don't look.*

Davi jumped to his feet. "We need to go," he demanded, his voice cracking in fear.

I seconded him and we ran, no longer uncomfortable from the silence and eeriness of the darklands, but horrified of *what* was watching and moving towards us.

Within a few meters, I felt the vines tighten around my chest. Davi screamed. It echoed through the lands as the thorns and brambles parted, tossing me out. I assumed his scream was when the vines took hold of him.

I landed on him this time, my chest falling over his back. The vines and trees may have allowed us to enter, but they surely didn't treat us as special. I rolled off him and stood, dusting the sand from my clothes. I hadn't realized the darklands ended where Navarin began. My eyes adjusted to the bright yellow light of day. Seafoam-colored sand stretched to a lavender, sparkling sea, and glitter danced in the air around us. Large, colorful shells of varying shapes moved in and out with the tide. A single pink shell slid on the wet sand then stopped. It was exactly as it had been described.

Davi pulled himself up. "How do we pass the sea?"

I glanced around, noting that other than a few trees with fan shaped leaves and large pink fruit there was nothing. "We walk." Hopefully if we followed the seashore, we will happen upon something.

"It's daylight. We'll be spotted."

He had a point, but unless we returned to the darklands we had no choice but to trek through the sand. I took my shoes off and stuffed them in my satchel, as walking in the fine sand was difficult in them.

Davi followed my lead, glitter dust falling in our hair and shoulders. It felt like we walked for hours before we came across fae. A small village, by the looks of the few structures fashioned from the trees, and the large leaves used as roofs. A handful of boats built from the leaves were scattered along the shore. They didn't see us as we hid behind one of the large trees with fan leaves.

Water dripped from a large leaf above our heads, causing the glittery fairy dust to run over our faces. It gave me an idea. The leaves were water repellent, and we were elves. The leaves were large enough to hold a person. If we hid until night, we could use them to push across the sea, hopefully finding a place to hide before morning.

We backtracked away from the fae, using the trees for cover. Communicating with plants was our specialty and the trees complied. They dropped large leaves we used for cover as we lay in the sand. Even elves needed sleep to recharge.

Through the crack between the leaf and the beach, the yellow sky changed to gold then filled with shades of purple until darkness swallowed it. Once the sun lowered, we crawled out from under the leaves. They tied themselves into knots by the stem, and we pushed the makeshift raft towards the sea. Fae covered the land, sea, and air and we didn't know, if caught, whether they'd be friend or enemy. It was important we stayed covered.

We pushed the raft into the warm water. Luminescent life glowed around us, mixed with glittery fairy dust. The makeshift raft lowered as I climbed in, but it stayed afloat. I asked the leaves to guide us to Verboten, realm of the trolls. So far, the plants had listened and protected us. We didn't have a choice but to hope they weren't taking us into trouble. Aradian plants were an elf's friend, but Navarin plants were foreign.

The only other choice we had was to stay on the seashore and walk all the way around Navarin. That wasn't much of a plan, as it would make the journey days longer and we'd surely get caught, as more small villages scattered the shoreline.

We didn't speak, as the sea fae below us might catch a word, nor did we move as the air fae may fly over and wonder about leaves jiggling. We did glance at each other from cracks between the top and bottom leaves.

It was a long night filled with unease as we floated where the current took us. Light streamed through cracks between the leaves, music and voices carried over the seas from what sounded like a celebration. Fairy dust rained down on us. Davi mouthed "festival of dust," his expression displaying it was more of a question then a statement. I dropped my shoulders, laying on my back, then turned my head, glancing at the sea, trying to see what was happening, but all I saw was glittery dust falling around me and a sea that appeared to stretch endlessly.

Neither of us was a fae expert but, as a subspecies of the fae, we learned some about their customs. The festival of dust was a sacred occasion when the fae celebrated death. The fae believe they turn into fairy dust in death. The dust blows over the realm, coating everything.

The sounds grew louder as we floated closer. Gently, I pressed my hands against the center of the top leaf, guiding it upwards, and rotated my head. The sea lifted in a wave, giving me enough of a boost to see seafoam sand where the lavender ended.

The realms were in the middle of a great war and the elves were celebrating. I let out a long, frustrated sigh then begged the leaves to carry us away from the island. Whooshing air blew the top leaf of the makeshift raft, exposing me long enough I caught a glimpse of dragons. Not fiery red and orange dragons, but white dragons in a V formation. I shivered – ice dragons. They weren't planning on burning Navarin, but freezing it as a solid chunk of lavender with Davi and I on top.

Chilly air spread over the top of the leaf as an army of them spread above the seas, below zero wind flowing from their mouths. I imagined everything freezing beneath them. The sea lifted the raft. I curled my fingers over the edge of the bottom leaf, no longer concerned about being spotted by a fae, but becoming an ice sculpture.

The raft lifted higher and higher, then plummeted into the sea, warm water covering me as I was pushed under the water's surface, scrambling to hold onto the leaf. The raft fell out from under us, forced downward from the wave. I struggled against the water, unable to swim, thinking that was it. My life was over. The great war had taken us captive.

I lost the ability to kick as something wrapped around my ankles, dragging me through the water. My back slid along the sandy bottom as the water became shallow enough I could lift my head, gasping for air.

Pulling myself onto the beach, blue seaweed untangled from my ankles and drifted back into the water. *Thank you.*

"Davi," I called; on my feet, glancing but not seeing him. A wave of frigid air crawled over my skin. "Davi!" I screamed, diving into the sand for protection, almost in a panic. We needed to get somewhere safe. Cries and screams pierced my ears as I crawled further onto the shore.

"Marya." A sandy hand covered mine. I turned my head to see Davi grasping my hands, trying to pull me upward. Next, we were running, cold air raising the hair on our backs, shrieks filling our ears. My head spun and my mind didn't process all that my eyes saw.

Questions circulated as we moved through the chaos. The cheerful music and song gone. *What happened in the time we were in the darklands? Had the fae angered the dragons? How long had we been in the darklands?* It felt like a day, but in darkness it was hard to tell one day from the next.

A front pocket of my pants vibrated and I remembered the bark. Matthia said I would know. I pulled it out and snapped it in two, stuffing a chunk into my mouth. "Don't swallow," I reminded Davi, handing him half. It's flavor sweet and spicy as I sucked on it.

Fae scrambled and ran everywhere. Not a single one paying any attention to two elves racing toward the trees. It was pandemonium. Lightning bolts shot upwards, ahead, and behind us, but not at us, as they were meant for the dragons. Unicorns stampeded towards us. Using my senses, I reached for Davi's hand and pulled him to the right. Sand from the unicorns' hooves blasted our legs as they galloped past us.

I dodged to the left to avoid getting trampled. Land fae had the ability to shift into unicorns, and I'd heard stories but never seen one. They were large, and colorful manes flowed from their heads, parted where their horn jutted out. Light streamed into the air as their horns illuminated. Their beauty commanded attention and I lost myself.

"I can't see you," Davi shouted as we crossed the treeline, bringing me to the present. His words not sinking in as I dodged powerful legs and hooves.

Without stopping, his warm hand still in mine, I glanced his way. I couldn't see him either. The bark. It made us invisible. It came to mind later that the elvarin used it to leave the darklands. If we were invisible, we could move unseen. We didn't need the trees to hide us.

*Get to the other side,* carried between the trees, urging us into the open. Invisible, we wouldn't be spotted.

Trees with vining branches moved; tiny pink buds blew off, coating the ground below. That was our path. "Follow me," I shouted at Davi as I let go of his hand and veered to the right without pausing. My feet trampling the small pink buds.

I stuffed the bark into the side of my cheek and sucked as we exited the cover of trees, dodging unicorns and frigid dragon breath and ice. Bright, feathered air fae circled the dragons. Their colors mesmerizing. I barely noted we were running uphill until I almost stepped off a cliff. Reeling on one leg, I dropped backwards.

"Marya," Davi's voice hollered as it moved farther away from me.

A splash hit the water below, but I couldn't see Davi. Either he was still invisible, or he'd gone below the surface of the sea. A ripple in the water showed where something had dropped. A shell of tree trunk floated toward the ripple.

*Jump,* called the trees, urging me on.

I closed my eyes and jumped, my body splashing into the water. I sank below the surface and bobbed upward as my head broke through the surface of the water.

I opened my eyes and saw daylight, my head bobbing above the sea as I pulled myself onto the husk of tree trunk that floated towards me.

"Marya," Davi said, grasping for my hands where the husk was forced downward.

I lifted a leg over the edge and pulled my body over the side. "Davi. You made it."

Before we could celebrate our lives, or orient ourselves, the water carried us in a great circle of spinning water. We were caught in the disturbance, something everyone was warned about. It was something spoken of between all the realms. No one knew where it went, but I guessed we were about to find out as the tree husk carrying us drifted closer to the middle.

*Swim towards the blue light,* the plants urged as the husk carrying us was forced downward. *Don't fight it.*

# 5

**f**resh air filled my lungs as I coughed and choked, catching my breath. The water sucked us under and pushed us upward into the air, as high as the tops of the trees. My heart stopped and my stomach fell as the water dropped us in seconds to ground level.

I caught my breath for the second time in a moment and turned to Davi. His eyes wide, fear and shock mottling his features. I swallowed hard. "We're OK. We made it. I think." The bark still in my cheek, I took it out and stuffed it into my pocket.

He nodded. His Adam's apple bobbed as he swallowed hard. "Marya. We aren't alone."

# The Origin

From the corner of my eye, I spotted movement. Turning my head slowly, I noted trolls encroaching on us. Everything happened so fast and now it was too late to run from them. They circled us, moving in closer, completely surrounding us.

I hadn't seen a troll before, but knew enough about their appearance; short stature, long tails with bright feathers. All had their swords drawn and pointed at us. Davi and I huddled together.

"Elves," a troll with green tail feathers said as he moved closer. "What are elves doing here?" His words filled with disgust.

Neither Davi nor I responded, mostly out of fear. The trolls weren't our friends. They sided with the lycans. I scanned our surroundings, Davi so close I felt his breath against my cheek. There were plenty of trees and plants, all green unlike Aradia, where leaves came in silver, lavender and blue as well, but none close enough to call on for help.

"I asked you a question," the troll demanded, poking the tip of his sword at Davi.

"Can you put those down?" I asked in a shaky voice.

The troll narrowed his eyes. "No, I can't put it down. You are elves in Verboten. Why?"

*Think of something!* I urged my mind as it went blank. I couldn't tell them I was on a mission to end the great war by defeating the Dragon King. Surely they'd kill us. Their swords were probably dipped in something toxic, like vampire blood or lycan venom. Maybe cured with dragon fire.

"Are you spies?" asked another with bright orange tail feathers. She narrowed her eyes and stared at us.

Davi stuttered, "We aren't spies… We dropped in, but we'll be going home to Aradia now if you could just point us in the direction."

The trolls moved closer. The tips of their blades inches from us. "We're taking you with us," said the one with green feathers. His tail moved over his shoulder and the feathers draped over his chest.

We couldn't move or run. This was it; we'd been caught. My mission ended before we even got to safety in Drakonia. Vampires weren't friends, but they were allies of the elves for the moment. I had to remind myself, finding two young elves alone, the vampires might turn on us for a taste of our blood.

The trolls secured our hands with metal cuffs that tightened around our wrists and marched us through the woods. Large, green trees everywhere, and the sky not blue, but ribboned in colors as they seemed to move across it.

"Don't think of speaking with the trees," one said behind me, the tip of his blade resting against my back. "This blade will disembowel you before you can get the thought out."

An elf didn't always need to speak with a plant for them to help us. I guessed he didn't know that. His threat was taken seriously, and I took my eyes off the trees to appease him, after all, he had the sword.

"Now tell us why you're really here and maybe we don't kill you before we get to the Liege." The Leige was their ruler. I was impressed we were important enough to see him.

All had happened so quickly my mind hadn't really processed, but the trolls were on the side of the lycans not the dragons. Not the elves either, but maybe the situation had an out. "We're on our way to Sier," I said.

Laughter filled the air, similar to the elvarin in the darklands. No one took two elf children seriously. "A couple of elves." They chuckled more; their blades still firmly planted at our backs.

"Are you planning on saving the dead? The prince died night before last."

That's why they attacked the fae. They hadn't sworn allegiance or chosen a side, and in the king's sorrow his temper flared when he learned they were planning on going through with their festival of dust. The celebration of the dead.

A green stream of light moved through the trees from the left and hit the troll in front of us in the shoulder. Instead of reaching a hand, his tail grabbed his shoulder as he grumbled in pain. He halted, his sword out. "Who's there?!"

The trolls stopped moving. A second beam moved from another direction, over my shoulder, and caught the troll behind me. She screamed in agony. I didn't know Verboten, or much about trolls, but I'd never heard of light beams falling from the sky or shooting through forests.

Davi and I stayed still as the trolls behind us moved forward, swords out, eyes searching the woods. "There, from the trees," shouted a troll with red tail feathers.

"Go find it!" the one with green feathers ordered.

More green beams shot from all around, hitting one then another, as the trolls rushed deeper into the woods after whatever was causing the beams, leaving Davi and I cuffed. We could run; our legs were free.

Out of the woods marched a girl, maybe ten or eleven. Her tail was short with green and yellow feathers, and she was smaller-boned and thinner than the trolls. Her ears were pointed like an elf. She didn't exactly look like a troll, I noted as she moved towards us. She pointed to the cuffs around our wrists and nodded.

"Who are you?" I asked as she undid the cuffs. They dropped to the ground with a soft thud, but that was all the sound I heard, as she remained quiet.

Her large, dark eyes met mine then shifted to Davi as she motioned for us to follow her. Davi and I glanced each other and shrugged. She did save us from the trolls so she couldn't be all bad. Massive red, orange, purple, and blue gemstones the size of furniture jutted upwards from the grassy knolls and flatter areas between the trees. In many ways, it was prettier than Navarin, more colorful, and the sky moved as the ribbons of color waved like flags blowing in the breeze.

After a half hour or so's journey, we reached a trella-like structure filled with animals. Some were like the unicorns, but without horns, others were thick and large, standing on all fours. She marched past the animals to a set of wooden steps. At the top of them was a loft.

It wasn't much, but was enclosed and surrounded in fluffy, dry grass that crunched beneath our feet. "I'm Marya and this is Davi," I offered, lowering my satchel to the floor. After the journey we'd been through, my shoulders needed a rest.

"Mer-a," she said, looking at me. It was obvious she didn't speak well.

"Marya."

She pointed to herself, "Emra." The word labored, as she carefully formed the syllables. I wasn't sure what she was saying. Rolling it over in my head a few times, maybe she was trying to say Amber or Ember. For the moment I left it at Emra.

"Davi," he stated his name. "We are on our way to Sier. Can you point us in the direction to Drakonia?" he asked.

Instead of laughing as everyone else had, she nodded then rubbed her belly and cupped her hand, putting it to her mouth.

"Yes, we are hungry. Thank you," I said. My belly, being reminded it hadn't eaten since the pika in the darklands, grumbled loudly.

She smiled as she bounded down the steps.

Davi dropped onto the dry grass. "Our mission is over. Didn't you hear them? The prince is dead. Why are we heading to Drakonia and not Aradia?"

I may have omitted a few things. The mission wasn't exactly to save the prince, but I didn't divulge that yet. After everything we'd been through in the past couple days, I didn't want him more upset. "There's more to the mission. We still have to stop the great war. It isn't over. You were there when the dragons tried to freeze Navarin. That was after the prince died... if he really did." I wasn't convinced in any way that he was actually dead because I didn't trust the trolls that captured us. If the war was over, they had no use for us. "And our homeland might be the next one to burn or freeze!"

Davi narrowed his eyes and studied me. "You are determined to get to Drakonia. The one thing that can kill a dragon is there. You'll never pull that off."

He read me like he always does. I was shocked I'd kept it from him this far. Defiantly, I folded my arms across my chest. "Sure I will. I have something that will promise undying power and eternal life. He won't pass it up."

Davi's eyes opened wide. He knew exactly what those words meant, and they were dangerous. "That's only a myth." Warning dripped like blood from his words.

"He doesn't know that," I countered.

The door opened below, and we grew quiet. Small footsteps sounded against the stairs. We relaxed as Emra appeared with a basket of fruit and vegetables.

Once our bellies were full, we fell asleep. Awakened only when the door opened below us and a couple or more sets of feet walked into the tall, wooden building.

My head on Davi's lap, I parted the dry grass and peered through the slats in the wood. I couldn't see much below us, mostly shadows.

I listened to the voices and words. They were searching for two elves. Guards. They had to be troll guards. I swallowed hard. Davi's heart pattered so hard it sounded like drums. Another man spoke. Emra's father, maybe, assuring them he hadn't seen any elves.

I jolted up and pushed the dry grass toward the wall, motioning for Davi to crawl through. I followed him and we bunched it around us. I did my best to keep my breathing light as heavy footfalls echoed on the stairs and crunched the dry grass. Through the strands, I spotted a green feathered tail, his voice familiar, like the one we encountered earlier. He was joined by another. I couldn't make out his tail feathers, but he had a beard, and a female I noted only by her voice as she never entered my vision.

"There's nothing here. We haven't seen any elves," the one with the beard said, his eyes drifted to the bundle of dry grass we hid behind, and for a second our eyes met.

Convinced, the three trolls went down the stairs and outside. That was close, we had to go. Dusting the dry grass off, I slung the satchel over my shoulder and was ready to leave when the door opened again.

I ducked, dropping onto the dry grass heap. Davi pulled me under, but we were too late. The bearded troll, his hand on the banister stared at us.

"Amber brought you here, didn't she?"

We nodded.

He lifted a leg onto the final step, but didn't move any further. "She's a hybrid, and so am I." His form changed in front of us. I blinked, unsure what I was seeing. His legs grew longer, muscles became more developed, and his tail vanished. "She can shift herself and others. That's how we survive. Come inside the hut. It's too dangerous for you to leave at night. Amber will guide you out tomorrow."

He wasn't angry or surprised. I wondered how often she brought home strays. It turned out her father was a lycan elf and her mother a troll fae. For years, they used their own shifting abilities to hide until Amber developed her skill enough she learned to manipulate it and shift others. They'd kept her hidden, even though rumors spread of a child who had incredible abilities. She was mostly mute and had incredible difficulty forming words. They thought it was due to being so mixed.

We ate a hearty soup for dinner; chunks of meat surrounded in a thick broth and plenty of vegetables. Candlelight bounced against the walls. "Thank you for not turning us in. We..." I glanced at Davi, who wore a sour expression. "I plan on stopping the great war."

No one laughed.

"Then you'll need Amber and her abilities. She can hide you as a troll and no one will be any the wiser," her mother said, pushing a loose strand of hair behind her pointed ear. Her tail feathers short, like Amber's, and bright pink. She didn't look exactly troll or fae.

Amber's father had more lycan features. He was smaller than the average lycan but had muscular arms and a broad chest. His pointy ears were the only feature that gave away his elf. Hybrids weren't common, and were mostly considered taboo, but it happened and they didn't truly fit anywhere.

I thought of Matthia. How his parents left him outside the darklands. He, too, was a hybrid, elf and elvarin. The darklands accepted him, took him and others in, not only giving them a place to grow up, but a family.

Amber showed us to a small room with a comfy enough bed. It wasn't made from the fine fabrics and textiles of Aradia, but it was soft.

The next day, after a hearty breakfast, we set out with enough food supplies to last us a few days. The path through Verboten wasn't short and we'd travel through highly populated areas.

# The Origin

To disguise us, Amber shifted us into trolls. It felt weird being so short and having a tail loaded with long, yellow feathers.

The disguises came in handy, as we marched through villages unnoticed. Three troll children didn't raise a brow. At night, we rested in the woods, covered and protected by the trees the first night of our journey. The colored ribbons in the sky moved above us, shining golds, fuschia and purples, blue, and shades of green. Stars shining through the colors added sparkle to the night sky.

In the day, the sun shone on the ribbons of coloring, spreading it like a rainbow over the land. The gemstones in the ground caught the colors of the sky and twinkled, shining various colors against the underside of the leaves.

The second night, we slept in the woods under the sky again, covering ourselves with fallen leaves, but woke in the morning to a chilly wind that had blown them away.

Dawn near enough, light spread over several tall, muscled lycans in their humanoid form surrounding us. I scooted closer to Davi, who stared at them wide-eyed.

One lowered his hood, revealing dark hair tied back in a ponytail, the sides of his head shaved, and a thick unruly beard. He narrowed his dark eyes and seethed. "Two elves and a hybrid traitor."

Unfortunately, Amber's magic didn't disguise us when she slept, that's why we used the leaves to cover us.

The three of us scrambled upwards, holding hands, and huddled close to each other.

The same lycan spoke. His words loaded with threat. "You're all coming with us."

Elves weren't without magic and abilities, and messing with an elf in a forest was dangerous business. A lycan could overpower us easily with brute force, and had keener predator senses that allowed them to hear better, see further, and with more detail. They had increased speed and agility, but elves made up for all those things, especially when surrounded by plants.

Channeling magic through Davi, I called on the roots. The ground rumbled beneath our feet and cracked around theirs. Their arms flailed as they fought to stay balanced, and Amber used her magic to send out an invisible barrier of magic that pushed them backwards against the trees. Branches wrapped around their middles and roots entangled their legs, rendering them helpless.

We didn't waste any time in running until we felt safely out of their reach and stopped to catch our breath.

"Can you shift us?" I asked.

# The Origin

She shook her head. That blast must have taken too much. Regaining our breath, we continued running. Amber pointed ahead. Through the trees, I barely made out a sandy area. Cool, dry air brushed my skin. The trees became sparse. It seemed we were free, as the realm became closer with each step.

As we crested a small, sandy hill, two lycans waited for us in wolf form. They were massive, large enough to harness and ride, with powerful legs beneath them. We skidded to a halt and my knees pushed into the sand as I dropped.

The sun ascending, but not high in the sky, a flash appeared from nowhere and a streak of silver came down on the lycans' heads, lopping them off. They rolled down the sandy hill and a teal light opened and swallowed us.

# 6

The vampire, Samuel he called himself, wore his hair trimmed short and his face clean-shaven. He was tall and slender. The cave walls were smooth, a sandy color, as if sand was shaped and molded.

He studied the three of us. "Two elves and a hybrid. A strange combination, but you weren't heading to Drakonia by accident."

I swallowed. "No."

"You all could have died back there, at the least become prisoners, if I hadn't saved you. Tell me, why is it you are here?"

I opened my satchel and reached my hand into the small hole I'd left in the lining. Ripping it, I pulled out the serenity fruit.

He lowered his chestnut-colored eyebrows. "A fruit… A serenity fruit. You are going to offer him eternal life but, instead, poison him. Clever."

He figured that out easy. I thought it was a genius plan and his seeming approval gave me more reason to believe it could work. "Yes."

"You'll need my help. The harvesters have threatened to damn Blood Falls. They won't take kindly to an elf passing through." When harvesters took souls, the blood was drained into Blood Falls that dropped into Blood River in the mountainous area between Drakonia and the harvester realm of Thraves.

If they damned Blood Falls, it would harm every realm. The vampires drink the blood, which is filtered through rock as it enters Verboten as clear water. It moves through each realm. Serenity Tree would wither. Without it, shortages would cause even more death. "You can portal us."

He brushed his fingers below his clean-shaven chin. "Not *us*. You, and you alone. The hybrid and her family will stay here in Drakonia, along with the elf. The king is self-serving enough to believe your proposal."

My blood pumped faster as the reality of my mission was coming to fruition and accepted as a good idea. So much for Davi's hesitance. I glanced his way and shot him a *'you see'* glance. He retorted with an eye roll.

Without portalling, as I guessed that used energy he wanted to conserve, we followed Samuel downhill to an underground vampire lair. I'd never been so close to so many at one time. It was a bit unnerving, even knowing they weren't planning on harming us. It wasn't only the pact between the elves and vampires that made me think we were safe, but Samuel explained they were loyal to their minister who would make sure no harm came to any of us.

What was a vampire promise worth? It was worth enough to at least accept his help and cross my fingers Amber and Davi would be safe. The vampires didn't pay us much mind as we followed him through the crowd. By actions, they displayed an elf or hybrid meal wasn't on the menu that day.

He brought us to a cavern room. The walls made of the fine light sand. Candlelit sconces on the wall shed enough light I was able to make out Amber's parents as they swallowed her in their grasp.

As if Samuel read my mind, he explained their lack of tolerance to daylight didn't preclude them from keeping tabs on what was happening in each realm. Word got out that two elves were traveling through Verboten and may have been collected by a hybrid with extraordinary powers. They maintained eyes and ears everywhere, and portalled Amber's parents as soon as they confirmed who we were.

Commotion in the large chamber filled with vampires forced my attention as I looked to Samuel for an explanation.

"Wait here," he commanded, in a voice most people wouldn't cross.

Not me. I'd come this far and wanted to know what was going on. From a safe distance of the doorway between the rooms, I watched as a vampire stood on a balcony cut from stone above the cavern. He wore a long cape made of fine elfin fabric. A ring on his finger curled over the stone caught my eye. It glinted red from the light of the chandelier.

He carried himself as important and had command in his voice: "Merla has summoned a representative from every realm and asked specifically for the hybrid causing so many problems."

My gut clenched as I turned my head to see Amber. She nodded and moved towards the doorway, leaving the safety of her parents' love. Standing in the large chamber, she said, "I... go…" and pointed to the vampire on the balcony then to herself.

Vampire heads turned and looked upon her, some with sympathy, others with relief. The important vampire on the balcony glided down a set of steps. The vampires parted as he moved towards her, finally stopping in front of her. He lifted his hands to her cheeks. "You are a brave girl. It is a large burden you bear. Your family will be safe."

# 7

The day Amber was sent to Navarin, Samuel portalled me with him to watch, insisting I take my satchel. The realm showed signs of the ice dragon battle. The beautiful trees, with their big, floppy leaves, hung in a sickly green from the ice and chill. The sea covered in glittery dust mixed with small chunks of wood and fragments. It was no longer lavender, but dark and agitated, as if someone had stirred a pot of sand.

The sea churned as a wave rose from it with a woman on top. Her long, lavender hair flowed in the breeze. A blue tulle dress met the top of the wave, her feet not visible. The wave stopped high in the air. She extended her arms as she addressed all those in attendance. "Too many have died in this war; parents, siblings, neighbors. Navarin is covered in the dust of our dead. How many have to die? How long do we have to keep fighting? It ends!"

She waved her hands in front of her, pointing at all in the crowd. "Bring me the hybrid girl causing so much trouble in Verboten."

Amber's parents walked to the edge of the sand. Merla's wave lowered and moved forward, hovering a meter from Amber and her family.

She put a hand under Amber's chin and lifted her head. "This is the girl you fear. A child! Nonsense. She will remain with me for the next forty-eight hours. At sunset, you will bring me six more hybrids, a unicorn horn, a harvester's eye, the wing from a dragon, the tip of an elf's ear, the tail of a troll, a vampire's fang, and from the lycan a heart, as they were the first to draw innocent blood."

Hushes and murmurs passed over the crowd as Merla offered Amber a hand and guided her onto the wave. It receded into the sea.

Samuel turned to me. His face solemn, his words urgent. "You must go immediately!"

In a flash, he opened a portal to Sier. Unwrapping the cloak over his shoulders, he draped it over mine then pushed a small vial into my hand. I curled my fingers around it. "Don't inject it until you are ready, or the fruit may wither and die," he warned.

I nodded.

With a look of confidence and well wishes, he ushered me through the portal. Immediately on the other side the chill hit my face and I wrapped the cloak tight around me to keep in heat, and pulled the hood over my head.

Spots of dark sand and rock poked through the thinner layers of snow. I uncurled my hand and glanced at the small vial containing a red liquid – vampire blood. I unrolled a scroll Samuel had tucked into my satchel before we left Drakonia. A map of Sier, with the path to the castle marked in red. The king's castle was on the tallest peak of the highlands.

The path there would be treacherous, as the mountainous terrain was filled with pitfalls and dragons. It wasn't a short journey. To get to the tallest peak, I had to go through the forest of whispers – that appeared at least a day's journey – and cross the Ejlan falls.

I still had some bark left from the darklands and placed that in the side of my cheek. The rocky terrain was better for flying creatures than those on foot, especially an elf who had soles made from the tough leaf of the baya tree. After a half day journey, my shoes were in tatters and my feet sore. I let out a small scream as a pointed rock pushed through my shoe and into my foot.

"Those aren't good shoes for the highlands. Try these," said a familiar voice. I glanced upward to see Matthia, a thick fur cloaked around him.

Shock didn't begin to describe how I felt seeing him. Once we left the darklands, I didn't think I'd ever see him again, yet here he was, offering me boots made from hide and solid soles made from the bark of the makan tree. The frigid air threatened to freeze the tears welling in my eyes. I stopped sucking on the bark and took the boots. "Thank you. How did you know?"

His soft lips curled into a smile. "An elf trying to save the realms was worthy of my curiosity. I've been following you, and you've caused quite a stir. The lower realms are all talking about the elves trying to stop the war."

Once I got the boots on, he pulled another piece of bark from his pocket and broke it in two. Handing me a piece he stuffed the other into his mouth. "The one you're sucking on is nearly worn. I could see you faintly."

"Thank you."

He glanced at the map. "It's quite a journey. At the rate you're walking, it'll take you three or four days to reach the castle.

There isn't much time, and we need to get you there quickly."

He was right. My feet were sore and bleeding. Every step hurt, but I was nothing if not determined. Mountains spread out before me, sparse with any shrubbery or plants. In the distance was the forest of whispers, the tall trees standing high in the air, their tops swallowed in the clouds. There didn't look to be an easier way to get anywhere but walk. "How?"

"I'm going to wrap my arms around you and fly. If you don't like heights, don't look down," he warned.

His arms snug around my middle, his wings flapped against the air as we rose off the ground. I closed my eyes, as looking down made me dizzy. Elves weren't meant to fly. The steady flap of his wings, the rhythm of his heartbeat against my back, and security of his arms, I felt safe enough as I sucked on the bitter bark. It wasn't flavorful in a good way, but kept us hidden.

We coasted down and, when my feet touched the ground, I opened my eyes. The forest of whispers behind us. We flew in sprints, as he couldn't fly high or carry cargo too far without stopping for a rest. We landed on a thick ledge outside the castle by nightfall. It was carved into the mountain.

We didn't start a fire to stave off the cold. Instead we used body warmth, as he curled his body around mine. We used the cloak Samuel had given me to cover ourselves. I barely noticed the cold as I fell asleep.

In the morning, after a meal of fruit, we crossed the gap between us and the castle. The drawbridge drawn, we flew over the high stone walls. Fresh bark in our mouths, we entered the castle. It was eerily silent. Two massive fire dragons stood outside the door to the inner chamber and throne room, their heads as large as my satchel. Their thick arms hung from broad, square shoulders. I gulped nervously, even though I knew they couldn't see us. We waited.

The doors creaked open, and a female dragon exited. We used that moment to slip through before the doors fell closed again. Matthia stayed with me; invisible, but with me. I didn't show myself until I reached the throne.

Two more dragons were posted inside the throne room; one at each door. The king was perched on a throne that was large enough to fit two elves comfortably, but the king took up the entirety. His long legs stretched in front of him, fur boots covering up to his knees, more fur draped his shoulders. An elbow against the arm rest of the throne, he leaned his head on his hand.

I took the bark out of my mouth, swallowed hard to give myself an extra boost of confidence, and walked around the chair, revealing myself to him. Each step difficult as my feet burned from the sores on them.

His steely blue eyes met mine and his face contorted in rage. "An elf!" The floor shook under the weight of his words.

I nodded. "I have something for you."

He guffawed and waved his hand. The guard closest us left his post and proceeded to wrap a single large hand around both my wrists.

I held my ground. "I have something the king will want."

The guard's voice, low and growly, said, "What could an elf possibly have for the Dragon King?"

He dragged me towards the door, but I wasn't done. It couldn't end like this. I had to appeal to his narcissism. "Your majesty I am a lowly elf not worthy of your presence, but the gift I have for you is great."

The dragon continued dragging me toward the door and stopped at the command of the king. "I'm curious. What could an elf possibly offer me?"

The dragon guard squeezed my wrists tighter. "I have fruit from Serenity Tree."

The king guffawed. "How did you manage that? It doesn't matter. Show me."

"I need my hands to do that."

The king waved a hand, and the guard unclutched my aching wrists. I reached into my pocket and pulled out the serenity fruit. Matthia held the vial of blood that he'd inject before the king ate. I felt his hand against mine. "This fruit offers you eternal life."

The throne groaned as the king stood and walked towards me. His eyes drooling over the fruit. He was vein and self-serving enough to believe an elf would offer him eternal life. Blood rushed through my veins faster with each step he took. "Give me that."

Trying not to show my nerves, I moved closer to him, leaving the guard near the door. "I can't just yet. No one can take the fruit of Serenity Tree from an elf unless the elf gives it willingly. The only way I'll give it willingly is if you call off the war." A bluff, 100%.

The king's large hand, the backside covered in fur, reached for the fruit, which I quickly positioned behind my back where Matthia could fill it with the vampire blood.

"You deny me!"

I swallowed the lump forming in my throat. "No. I only hope to make a bargain so the realms can be at peace again."

He narrowed his eyes and brushed a furry hand against his fiery red beard then laughed. "You want to offer me eternal life to stop the war."

"Yes."

His laugh cut off as quickly as shutting a door, and his tone changed. It became filled with malice and hate. As he said the words, I knew he didn't mean them. Once he had the fruit, he'd continue doing what he was doing, reneging on the deal. "Fine. We have a deal. I will stop the war. The realms can go back and Merla can stay at the bottom of the Lavender Sea where she belongs."

I pulled my hand in front of me but didn't uncurl my fingers wrapped around the fruit. "I give the fruit to you willingly, with a warning. If you don't live up to your word, you will die."

"Fine, fine." He was anxious.

His actions proved to me I was doing the right thing. He didn't mean a word, and neither did I. Everything I told him, I'd made up. There was no truth, except the fruit of Serenity Tree is said to give eternal life, but no one's ever eaten it to prove it. Mostly it's lore.

Dragons have super-sensitive hearing, so Matthia brushed my hand as our clue that the vampire blood was injected into the fruit.

I uncurled my fingers and pushed my hand towards the king for him to take the fruit. Immediately, he stuffed the little fruit into his mouth and savored it. Within moments, he went pale. He began changing into a dragon, but only partially. His face bloated, claws formed instead of hands, and a large white wing exploded from his back. He dropped head long, face planting on the stone floor.

"You poisoned him!" The dragon guard roared so loud the walls shook and I had to dig in my heels to keep from falling over.

I stuffed the bark into my mouth.

"You will die!" the guard shouted as my figure vanished from his sight.

The king's sword lay awkwardly against him, the hilt pointing towards me. I grabbed it and stumbled under its weight. The dragon guard closed the distance between us as arms came around me and helped steady the hefty sword. I screamed, "No. The fruit knows his heart and his word was untrue. He killed himself."

The dragon guard dove toward me after hearing my voice, but missed. We brought the sword down, slicing off the king's wing. It was heavier than I expected as I clutched the side, much of it dragging on the ground. It was, alone, as large as myself. "I'm bringing this to Merla."

The dragon skidded to a stop. "You can't have that."

"Would you prefer a sacrifice from the living?" I snarled, dropping the sword. It plunked against the stone floor.

The door opened and more dragons rushed in. Matthia wrapped his arms around me and lifted me into the air and through the king's personal flight hole.

# The Origin

We stopped at a small cave and climbed inside. Peering into the blue sky, it quickly filled with winged dragons exiting from holes throughout the highlands.

"The dragons are leaving. Evening will be here soon. I can't take you with me. It would take too long to carry you and the wing." Matthia narrowed his eyes and glanced it with disgust. "But I must go to Navarin and see what Merla does. You stay here in the cave. It's too small for a dragon and, if you suck the bark, they won't see you. I'll return soon." He pulled another chunk of bark from his pocket and handed it to me.

I curled my legs to my chest and draped the cloak around me for warmth. The night was cold, but a fire would give away my spot. I sucked the bark on and off. Too afraid to fall asleep, I huddled there until Matthia returned in the early morning.

Merla mixed the sacrifices together, transforming them into a liquid she had each hybrid, including Amber, drink then warned everyone: "The transformation will begin immediately, but you have three days to go back to the realm where you belong. After three days, veils will separate the realms. The only land where anyone can go will be where all realms meet. These seven are the only ones who can walk between realms. These Realm Walkers are to be liaisons for disputes between the realms. They can marry anyone they want, but their first intercourse will lead to a Realm Walker so each successive generation has a replacement. If any harm ever comes to any of them or their ancestors, the realms will fall, and war will replace peace."

There was only one thing on my mind. "How do we get home in three days?"

Matthia dropped his eyes then lifted them to meet mine. "You are brave and beautiful. You made this perilous journey and killed your mark. We will make it home if we go the route where the realms meet."

It would be a dangerous journey, but not more so than what I'd already lived through to get to Sier. We flew mountain top to mountain top, dodging dragons. We had very little rest, but managed on the third day to reach the center where all the realms came together. I spit out the bark, I hoped for good. I held out my hand. "You don't need it either."

He pushed my fingers back. "I can't. My ugliness is my shame."

"You aren't ugly, but beautiful. I couldn't have managed this without you. You are kind and gracious. I want to see your face."

Reluctantly, he spat out the bark, revealing himself. He was beautiful. I reached my hands to his face and stood on my tiptoes as I kissed his lips.

# The Origin

He backed away, surprised, then read my face and pressed his lips against mine. My heart exploded in fireworks as I wrapped my arms around his neck and buried myself in the kiss.

# EPILOGUE

The journey through the area where all realms met wasn't filled with treachery. Merla's spell transformed the land. Trees filled with colorful leaves made a circle around a field of grass. The air warm like spring, and the scent free of death. It was fresh and new.

The great war ended, and the realms divided. Amber stayed in Drakonia with her family as their Realm Walker. Merla got all the credit, but it was the king's death everyone celebrated as we rebuilt our realms.

I've written the story as I remember to pass on the truth of how two elves, a hybrid, a hybrid from the darklands, and a vampire, killed the King of Dragons. Years will pass and people will forget, but my children will pass on to their children the story: from one generation to the next.

# REALM WALKER

# Accidental Ghost
## Soul Catcher Vol. 1

# 1

Halloween came every day for me since I fell into a river of blood in a realm I'd never heard of. It was innocent. I was spelunking when I dropped through a cavern and into Blood River. Terra a hybrid saved me. She even got me back home after I was kidnapped by vampires and escaped to Thraves, land of the harvesters where I met death and learned my destiny. Sometimes I'd give my soul to return to my former life.

I dropped the pickaxe. I wouldn't get the hang of it. The pick wasn't working for me.

I glanced at my trainer in his spirit form.

"I'll never get it right."

"You will."

"I'm your punishment, aren't I?" He was a prominent tribunal representative for the Harvester realm of Thraves before I dropped into his realm spelunking.

"No. My punishment is being kicked off the tribunal because of my own actions."

There were eight realms all of them represented on the tribunal except the human realm or Lols for Land of Lost souls. They called us commoners. We were anything but common and I resented being called common.

"We'll try again tomorrow."

"Sure," I climbed the steps to the brownstone. He vanished into the night. His spirit returning to Thraves. Harvesters could only harvest souls in Lols in spirit form. I had a beef with this realm being called that. Souls here weren't lost we were home on Earth or wherever it was. As a harvester hybrid I could harvest in my physical form.

I rolled the rocks from each realm between my fingers. I was a hybrid of five realms; Verboten, Aradia, Sier, Canida and Thraves meaning I was a troll, elf, dragon,

# The Origin

Lycan and harvester hybrid. According to death I not only had to collect a rock from each realm but had to enter it which I had. I didn't know what good the Drakonian rock did since I wasn't vampire but death insisted it was useful. She was cryptic.

I bore the mark of each realm on my chest. A passport that allowed me to enter and exit any realm I was part of.

Harvesting wasn't a perfect science and Metford, my instructor and were learning together. Evidently harvester hybrids weren't common.

That was six months ago. I had improved in the art of harvesting but still had some troubles.

The dark soul latched onto my pickaxe and wouldn't let go. I hit the end on the ground, hoping to jar it lose but it clung like sticky goo.

"Easy, don't let frustration get you."

Easy for him to say. Metford was born in Thraves and designed for harvesting. I held the pickaxe upward like he'd taught me, the black ball rose finally. It was ascending to the otherworld. The place dark souls go.

No, no, no I screamed in my head as a tiny piece of it stuck. It looked like a black blob of stretched slime. The yellow stone in the eye of the pickaxe flashed.

One of the rocks used to trap the souls was blinking in and out. When a soul was trapped, they shone bright, connecting in a six-point star. I kept the pickaxe steady as I maneuvered myself to the rock then carefully lowered myself.

I kept the pickaxe stable as I could with one hand, lowered myself and touched the rock. Its energy returned and the pesky dark soul continued its ascension as the tiny stuck piece became unstuck.

I dropped the axe and sighed.

"You're improving," Metford said in a congratulatory tone.

I held up my hand to high five but his spirit hand went right through mine.

# 2

My eyelids drooped as I worked to keep them open. Taking another gulp of my double shot iced coffee wasn't enough. Harvesting and early morning classes didn't work but it was the only time this class was offered.

Dr. Blyzbub took her glasses off, twirling them in her hand as she spoke. "Vickery House in upstate New York is an example of spirit attachment to a structure. Several families moved in and were scared out after complaints of paranormal events. The families all lived ghost free lives after leaving. It has been said the house could be a gateway between the living and the dead. The house has been unoccupied since 1947."

# Realm Walker

Thanks to being a harvester, I now had a double major; paranormal studies and geology which meant sleepless nights for the next three years. Adding paranormal studies meant more classes. Therefore, I take a class at eight in the morning instead of sleeping. Dr. Blyzbub was full of stories of hauntings. This weekend I'd check out Vickery House.

I searched it on my laptop and saved the address. It was in the town of Blake. A small quintessential town with cobblestone streets and mom and pop locally owned shops.

Vickery House put it on the map. They don't do tours in the house but it is part of a tour of Blake.

I stuffed my laptop into my bag and pulled it over my shoulder. It was time to go home and sleep before tonight's harvesting.

"How about a coffee?" Sharae asked.

She was hot, sweet and had been flirting with me since the beginning of the semester but I didn't have time to date and I had a thing for a girl I hadn't seen in months – Terra.

The girl who saved me in Drakonia. What we had was an attraction and hadn't gone beyond a couple kisses but I couldn't get her out of my mind.

Our destinies weren't intertwined. I was stuck here harvesting and she was saving the realms.

# The Origin

It was time to move on but not today. My bed was calling. "Thanks but not today. I had a late night," her face dropped as the words left my mouth. I'd turned her down so many times.

Her deep brown eyes turned downward, "sure, another time."

I felt like roadkill driven over by many cars.

I liked her. What wasn't to like. She had the right size curves, a sweet smile, a caramel complexion, endless brown eyes and was interested in the dead.

My alarm went off, it's annoying ring blasting in my ear. I chose it so I'd wake up. Rings that weren't obnoxious became part of my dreams and I slept through them.

I slid the ringer off instead of snooze and got up. My stomach complaining about being empty. A side-effect of being a full-time student with a double major and moonlighting as a harvester was never having time to shop or do laundry. I pulled on a pair of sweats that smelled freshish and slipped on a pair of shoes.

The beauty of living in New York was food was always close.

I picked up all the clothes on my floor and tossed them into a bag with soap pods and dryer sheets. There was a laundromat on the corner before the coffee shop.

After tossing my clothes in the machine I walked next door and ordered a ham and cheese croissant and double shot iced coffee.

I turned on my computer and continued my research of Vickery House.

It seemed a pretty typical haunting, an unrested dark soul. Noises like scraping against the floor and even in the heat of the summer a specific room was chilly.

Wait, maybe not so typical. A young couple bought the house in the spring of 1946. His niece came to live with them after her mother died. Soon she started talking to herself, carrying on conversations that escalated into her sleepwalking and eventually the girl refused to go back into the house. She interacted with the spirit. Maybe she was a harvester hybrid too. She went home to her father but the nonsense didn't stop and eventually she killed herself.

Spirits of unrest generally went about their business the day they died, repeating it day after day. This one hadn't.

No one ever died in the house but its occupants always complained of the same things, strange noises and a freezing room. Of course anyone who ever lived in the house was dead and no one ever died in the house.

I finished my clothes, returned to my brownstone and showered.

# The Origin

Metford's voice entered my head from the comicay, a gel device that fit above the wrist. The harvesters gave it to me. It was used for communication among other things.

Our meeting place tonight was the Midnight Sugar Company in Dublin Ohio.

The elevators or gateways made it much easier to travel the land of the living and get there quickly. They were a static disturbance, found often times in cemeteries but not always. As a harvester who saw spirits the ones in cemeteries were the easiest for me to find. They allowed me travel anywhere in Lols. I stepped in and thought of where I was going. The elevator vanished as I stood on the sidewalk outside the candy store. A large sign was outside the storefront. On either side of two lollipops were the words Dublin Ohio. Beneath that Midnight est. 1952 and beneath that Sugar Company.

Did someone fall into a vat of chocolate and drown or eat too much taffy?

Metford appeared at my side. He was tall and thick with a goatee he was always tugging at as I was in the middle of harvesting. It was a nervous habit and lately he didn't tug so much. I was getting better.

"A honeymooning couple died in the hotel across the street in 1993. It was a double homicide, and the killer was never apprehended."

I never asked where he got his info. My eyes swept the hotel. It was several stories high.

"It was in rm. 513."

*Great.* Metford stayed at my side filling me in on the details of the couple's death as I strolled into the hotel.

Situated on the left was a large circular check in counter. To the right were plush sage colored couches and chairs and wooden tables. A large mural of a river and woods in a modern style was painted on one wall.

The clerk at the counter smiled as I walked past him as if I was a guest returning from dinner. No one but me could see Metford as he was in spirit form. Sometimes I forgot and talked back to him. I got strange looks when that happened.

I pressed the button and waited as the elevator descended and the doors opened.

I didn't really have a plan but was hoping the room would be empty.

I knocked on 513 and didn't get an answer. That was good. I slid the stone from Sier over the card pad and the door unlocked. Each stone did its own special thing.

Once inside I dropped my harvester bag onto the bed. It was a Coach I found at the secondhand shop. I guessed its previous owner got rid of it for the next years style. It worked. I looked inconspicuous and the pickaxe fit into it nicely without catching any eyes.

I placed the rocks at equal points in the middle of the room after rubbing them together in my hands. The process recharged them. I grabbed the pickaxe and waited.

The couple had returned about nine according to the night clerk. Their screams were heard about an hour later. It was 8:56.

At 9:07 the couple came in kissing. Their hands all over each other. Clothes dropped to the floor and I turned. They were dead but it still felt an invasion of their privacy. Not really a horrible thing to make love every day before dying. I'd seen worse in my six months of harvesting.

I let the rocks do their thing as the couple's spirits coalesced into the center of the rocks.

I touched the female as she was closest. Her soul shining white on the pick. I brought it upward and watched as her spirit ascended. I then touched the man's soul, also white, both pure souls, and raised it.

The door opened. Fudge! I looked to Metford like he could help but as a spirit there was nothing he could do.

The man's spirit ascended. It would have been an easy job. Pure souls usually were.

A tall man stared at me, his mouth gaping. I guessed he'd never seen a 19-year-old with a pickaxe in a hotel. He looked like a businessman with his expensive suit, short, combed back wavy hair and clean-shaven face. By his unsteady gait it appeared he'd had a few too many to drink as he stumbled towards me and fell.

I tried to slip out of the way but couldn't in time as his shoulder dropped into my arm that held the pickaxe.

In a panic I flipped him over with my free hand and sighed relief when it had only grazed him. Dribbles of blood bubbled around the wound.

"Leave him." Metford said, tugging his goatee so hard I thought he'd pull it out.

"I can't. He's hurt."

"You're here to harvest souls. He'll heal from the injury."

Sure he would but I couldn't leave him like that. I ran to the bathroom and wet a washcloth and pressed it against his arm until the bleeding stopped.

Metford grumbled something as I rummaged around the man's cosmetic bag in search of bandages.

At the bottom of the bag and looking as if they'd been in the bag for years. The wrappers discolored and wrinkled were two regular size adhesive bandages. I ripped the wrappers off and pressed them over the wound.

"Since you interfered and shouldn't have, don't leave anything at the scene." Metford scolded.

I wore gloves, always. They were part of my kit. I lashed back at him, "What if he had died? How can you be so cold?"

I collected the rocks and put them back into the velvet bag I kept them in then the pickaxe and last I rolled up the bloody washcloth and tossed it in the bag.

"I'm not uncaring," Metford claimed as if trying to convince himself.

"What would I have done if he'd died besides harvest his soul?"

"That didn't happen."

"But what if it had?" I imagined myself with a murder rap. I'd be guilty with no excuse. I was sure harvesting souls wouldn't count as an excuse for an accidental murder. I'd be laughed out of court and sentenced, or I'd have to plea.